"Only a friend and a giraffe would stick his neck out for you."

-Jarod Kintz

I wish to dedicate this opus to my ever-loving niece, Dana Price, without whose determination and talent it would never have left my archives and to all the great grandchildren of the Price/Scott clan.

-Patricia Price Scott

www.mascotbooks.com

Pooh to the Flu Blues

For more information, please contact:
Mascot Books
620 Herndon Parkway #320
Herndon, VA 20170
info@mascotbooks.com

Library of Congress Control Number: 2015936801
CPSIA Code: PRR1117B
ISBN-13: 978-1-63177-162-0

Printed in the United States

Pooh
to the
Flu Blues

written by
Patricia Price Scott

illustrated by
Dana Price

Georgia Giraffe
Was a gas and a half.
She played and cavorted
and made her friends laugh.

Her pals in the jungle
thought she was a ball,

she could always amuse them
'cause she was so tall.

The small ones would ride
on her head for the view
which from way up there
seemed somewhat askew.

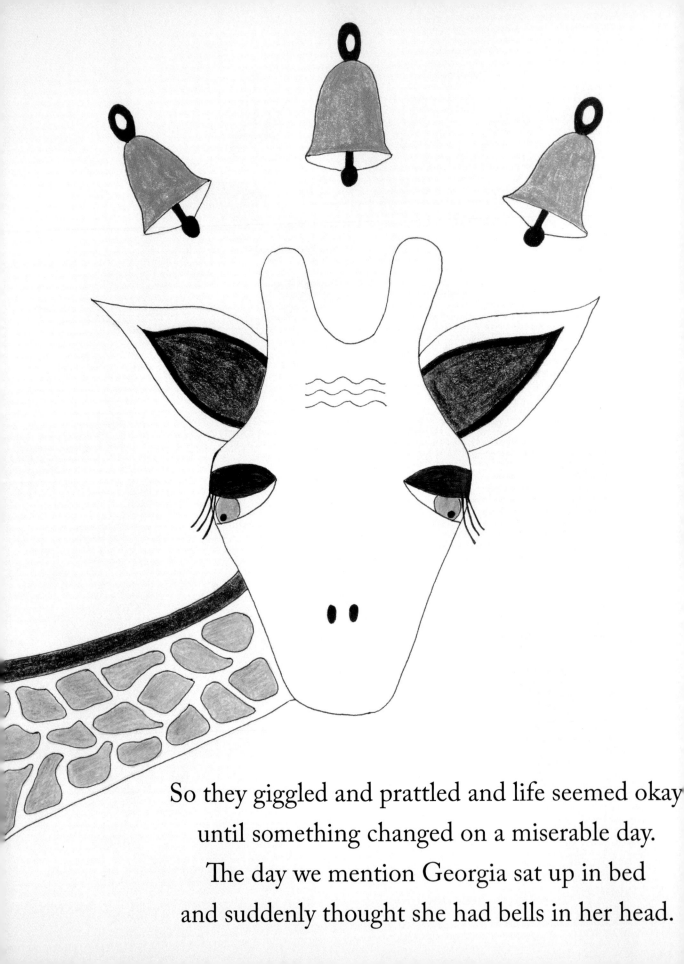

So they giggled and prattled and life seemed okay
until something changed on a miserable day.
The day we mention Georgia sat up in bed
and suddenly thought she had bells in her head.

Her long back delivered a terrible ache;
she moved herself slowly and thought it would break.

Her nose was plugged up
and her eyes were all bleary
and her whole body felt
so incredibly weary
that she wondered,
What is this from out of the blue?
and suddenly realized
she'd been caught by the flu.

As she chalked up her symptoms
she thought, and I quote,
The worst of this hurt
is my very long throat.
She shivered and shuddered
and shook like a wreck,
she had given new sense
to a pain in the neck.

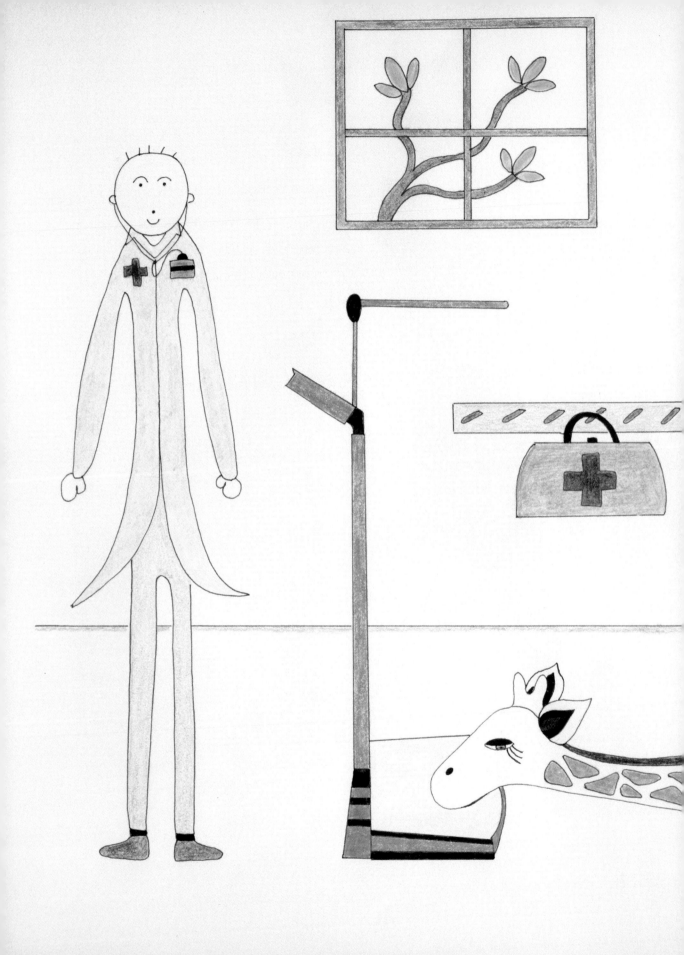

"I must get it together
and get to the doc
before I get worse—
I might go into shock!
It's going to be tough—
I might have to crawl…
but everyone knows
he won't make a house call."

When finally she got there
and told of her pain
the doctor looked thoughtful
and tried to explain
that if she were a monkey,
a cow, or a goat
perhaps he could give her
relief for her throat.

"You see, my poor Georgia, it's hard to dispense
appropriate care for a space so immense.
I'm sorry there's nothing to tell you to do,
for medical science can't fix up the flu."

So she wrapped up her neck
in a twenty foot shawl
and struggled back home
where she hoped to forestall
any dire complications
that still might befall.

Meanwhile her friends
had assembled en masse
to discuss what appeared
to be an impasse.
They thought, they conjectured,
but they said that they knew
there was nothing to help
a giraffe with the flu.
"But we really must try," they agreed at the end,
"For Georgia is clearly our very best friend."

The porcupine said that he'd part with some quills;
perhaps acupuncture would help with her chills.

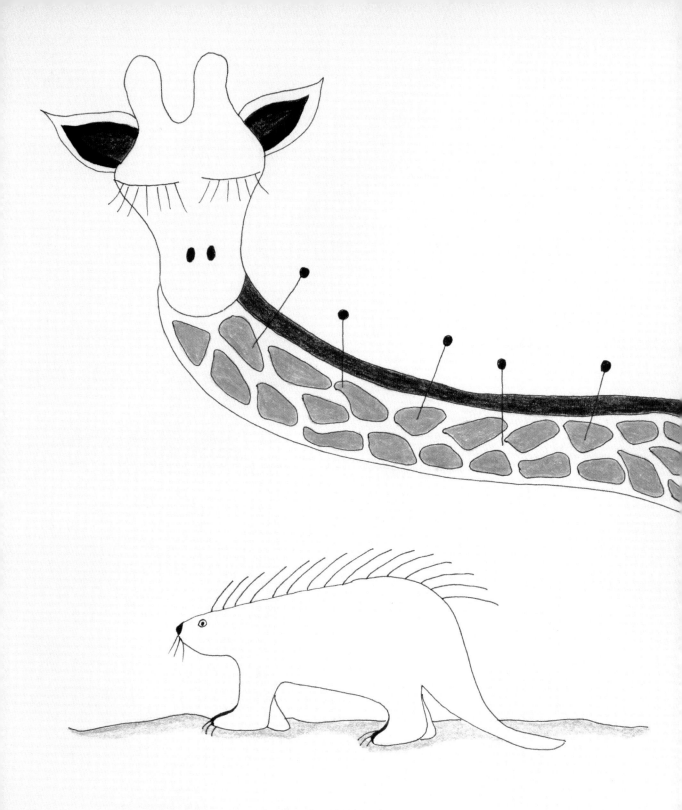

The skunk mentioned shyly that his scent had its minuses,
but that maybe its power would clear up her sinuses.

"I can't think of specifics," said Gonzo Gazelle,
"but if we tell her we love her, I know she'll get well."
And all of the others offered to do
whatever they could for Georgia's flu.

So they all got together and went as a group
and told their dear friend that she'd have to recoup.
They knew that they'd knock that old flu for a loop
'cause they had a bucket of hot chicken soup.

And so she got better
and soon was okay,
though her legs were quite wobbly
and got in her way.

The moral is clear for giraffes and for you,
if somebody loves you, say pooh to the flu.

About the Author

Word play is fun and when you are from a family that manipulates the language competitively, you play too. Christmas cards, birthday wishes, and graduations are usually observed with a bit of doggerel and a photo or sketch. That I am 96 hasn't seemed to alter this proclivity. Georgia is one result of such activity. A little rhyming for kids will also amuse the parents who have to read it. And Georgia's conformation, i.e. a very long neck, asks for it.